LIGHTNING!
AND THUNDERSTORMS

LIGHTNING!
AND THUNDERSTORMS

by Mike Graf

SIMON SPOTLIGHT

ACKNOWLEDGMENTS

The publisher is grateful to the following individuals for permission to reproduce their photographs and drawings:

Cover and photo insert: Alan R. Moller
Drawings by Tova Reznicek

Special thanks to the following for permission to use the first-hand accounts found in chapter five: Tim Gibson, Nathan Loyet, and the Lightning Strike and Electric Shock Survivors International (LS&ESSI).

SIMON SPOTLIGHT
An imprint of Simon & Schuster Children's Publishing Division
1230 Avenue of the Americas
New York, New York 10020
Manufactured in the United States of America
First Edition   10 9 8 7 6 5 4 3 2 1
Graf, Mike.
Lightning! and thunderstorms / Mike Graf.
        p.   cm.
Includes index.
Summary: Provides information and safety tips relating to lightning and thunderstorms.
ISBN 0-689-82018-6
1. Lightning—Juvenile literature. 2. Thunderstorms—Juvenile literature.
[1. Lightning. 2. Thunderstorms.] I. Title.
QC966.5.G7 1998
551.56'32—dc21
98-5158 CIP
AC

CONTENTS

The Drama of Lightning and Thunderstorms

Suddenly a large flash of light brightens the sky. *Kaboom!* It is followed by a loud clap of **thunder**. Scary, but not unusual. **Lightning** occurs all over the world. In fact, about 2,000 **thunderstorms** are happening at this very moment. In all, 16 million thunderstorms occur each year.

Lightning is exciting and beautiful to watch. Just like people's fingerprints, no two bolts of lightning are exactly alike. Don't get too close, though. The electricity from a lightning bolt is one of the most powerful forces on earth.

Did You Know?

One flash of lightning can have as much as one billion volts of energy. That bolt would be brighter than 10 million light bulbs of 100 watts each. People's eyes have been damaged from watching lightning at too close a range.

The sound of thunder can be startling, even scary. But don't worry. By the time you hear thunder, the danger of lightning has most likely passed. Until the next strike, that is. Usually we hear thunder a few seconds after we see the flash of lightning.

A Mythic Reputation

People have been fascinated by thunder and lightning for thousands of years. Throughout history, cultures have explained it in a variety of ways. Many ancient peoples believed good and bad weather was their gods' way of punishing or rewarding them.

The Ancient Greeks who lived between the fifth and second centuries B.C. believed lightning was used by the gods as a weapon. According to Greek mythology, Zeus, the greatest god of all, threw lightning bolts during battles. Both the ancient Greeks and later the Romans built their temples on land that had been struck by lightning because they believed the ground had become sacred.

In Scandinavia, according to the myths of the Vikings who traveled the world in the ninth and tenth centuries, Thor, the god of thunder and lightning, threw his favorite weapon, a hammer, at his enemies. As the hammer flew through the sky it created lightning. The rumble of thunder was Thor's chariot rolling across the sky.

In Europe during the Middle Ages many people thought lightning was created by evil spirits. By ringing church bells they believed they could scare away these spirits and keep lightning from striking their villages. Ringing bells was a dangerous job. The towers were usually the highest buildings in towns and therefore the most vulnerable to lightning strikes. In some parts of medieval Europe, people "fought" storms by rattling their swords or shooting off volleys of arrows into the sky.

Navajo Indians had a different explanation for lightning and thunder. They believed that lightning was made by the flashing feathers of Thunderbird, a mystical bird, and that thunder was produced by the bird's flapping wings.

A Really Big Spark

Benjamin Franklin is famous for his experiments with electricity. Perhaps his most famous took place in 1743 when he flew a kite into the middle of a thunderstorm. When he tied a key to the end of the kite string and the string became wet with rain water, a spark jumped from this key to another key Franklin was holding in his hand. The spark looked just like the sparks he had created in other experiments involving electricity. Franklin concluded thunderstorms must contain electricity. He further concluded that lightning was a huge spark of electricity in the air.

Remember, flying a kite during a thunderstorm is very dangerous, and many people have been killed trying to copy Franklin's kite experiment. Franklin himself was knocked unconscious more than once during his many experiments with electricity.

Kaboom!

Over the ages thunder has interested people as much as lightning. Some early Romans thought thunder was the sound created when two clouds bumped into one another.

Now we know that lightning causes that booming sound. Although it sounds as though thunder happens after lightning, actually the two happen at the same time. We hear thunder later because light travels so much faster than sound. Sometimes, thunder happens right after we see lightning, other times it happens several seconds later. The shorter the time between the flash of lightning and the sound of thunder, the closer the listener is to the lightning.

Forecasting a Storm

Scientists who study the weather are called **meteorologists**. Many study weather in order to forecast, or detect ahead of time, what the weather will be. Meteorologists use many different methods to help them, from simple human observation to complex computers.

Among other things, meteorologists warn people about dangerous weather conditions, such as severe thunderstorms. A warning may be issued if strong storms are moving toward an area. A severe thunderstorm "watch" means that current conditions could cause dangerous weather.

In addition to radar, weather experts use photographs taken from satellites in outer space, maps of lightning strikes, and computers to put all the information together.

Storm Chasers

Most people try to avoid dangerous storms. However, there are people called **storm chasers** who try to get as close as possible to turbulent weather. Typically they travel for miles chasing and tracking **tornadoes**, hurricanes, lightning, and more.

Some pilots actually earn their living by

flying right into storms to see firsthand what's going on. Other people chase storms in their cars.

One of the most famous storm chasers is a man named Warren Faidley. He has been fascinated with thunderstorms all his life. He chases over one hundred storms a year and takes spectacular photographs which have been published in books and shown in television commercials and movies.

In 1987 Warren was knocked to the ground by a lightning bolt. He still managed to take a picture. Once he filmed a tornado less than a mile from his car. Another time softball-size **hail** pounded his "Shadow Chaser," which is what he calls his car.

Even though Warren has been in dangerous storms, he plans his chases very carefully. Safety is of utmost concern.

Cloud Formations

Have you ever watched clouds on a summer day? Sometimes the clouds are small. At other times they're huge. In fact, clouds can reach heights of 60,000 feet—that's twice as tall as Mt. Everest! The large, puffy giants are thunderheads that can produce violent weather.

Where Warm Meets Cold

In order for thunderstorms to develop, warm temperatures are necessary. Many thunderstorms occur near the equator because the land and ocean on or near the equator receive the most direct sunlight. The Indonesian island of Java, which is very close to the equator, typically experiences thunderstorms 223 days out of the year—that's more than any other place on Earth. Southern Florida averages ninety thunderstorms a year, which is more than any other place in the United States. The southeastern United States and the Plains states also experience many thunderstorms because warm, moist air moves up from the Gulf of Mexico. The Pacific Coast rarely gets thunderstorms because the air there is drier and cooler.

The Right Stuff

Certain weather conditions must occur in the **atmosphere** in order for thunderstorms to form. Think of these as ingredients in a recipe. Just as you need the right foods and spices to cook something properly, thunderstorms need the right conditions.

Here's what thunderstorms need:

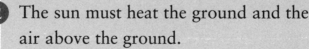

1. The air must be humid, which means it has a lot of moisture or water vapor in it.
2. The sun must heat the ground and the air above the ground.
3. This warming causes the air to become unstable, which means the air moves around and rises.

The Life of a Thunderstorm

There are three stages in the development of a typical thunderstorm. In the first the ground, which has been heated by the sun, warms the air directly above it. This air rises and carries with it water vapor. As the air rises, more air moves in below, is heated by the warm ground, and rises (see Figure 1).

In the meantime, when the rising air reaches what's called the dew point, the water vapor condenses, forming water droplets. **Cumulus** clouds now form. The updraft carries some of the water droplets even higher to a freezing altitude whereupon these droplets become ice crystals. As this process continues, the cloud grows in size until it's a large thundercloud, called a **cumulonimbus**.

At the second stage, the water and ice crystals grow heavier and heavier until the updraft can no longer support them. They fall to the ground as either rain or hail—irregular balls of ice that are formed when drops of water are repeatedly frozen (see Figure 2). Wind blows the drops up higher and higher to where the air is cold enough to freeze them. Then through many cycles of traveling from the lower to the upper part of the thunderstorms, many layers of ice develop, causing the hail to grow. When they're too heavy for the wind to

Figure 1   Figure 2   Figure 3

hold them up any longer, they fall out of the clouds and down to earth as hail. Lightning and thunder are frequent during this part of the storm. Strong winds can also develop. These huge thunderclouds are dangerous!

In the third stage, the falling rain or hail creates a downdraft that overwhelms the updraft —hence cutting off the source that's been feeding the storm. The thunderclouds start to fade and the storm ends (see Figure 3).

TRY THIS only if supervised by an adult

Create your own miniature weather system! Ask an adult to boil water in a teakettle. Then have him or her take the kettle off the stove when it's steaming and, while wearing gloves, hold a metal pie plate full of ice a few feet above the steaming kettle. Turn off the lights. Shine a flashlight right underneath the pie plate. Clouds will be forming there! The bottom of the pie plate will also be dropping water like rain. This is because the warm, moist air is hitting the cooler air, right at the pie plate. That's where the air becomes saturated, or heavy with more water than it can hold.

Nature's Spectacular Sound and Light Show

Just as Benjamin Franklin showed with his experiments, a bolt of lightning is really just a huge spark in the sky.

There are two kinds of electricity. One is current electricity, which flows or moves from one place to another. This is the kind of electricity that travels through electric outlets in our homes and lights our lamps and runs our televisions and refrigerators. The other kind is called **static electricity**. Static electricity doesn't move, it stays in one place. But it is attracted to or repelled by static electricity in other objects.

Lightning is caused by static electricity in thunderclouds.

How Do You Find Static Electricity?

Static electricity is created, for example, when you rub a balloon back and forth across your hair a number of times. As you pull the balloon away, your hair moves with it. What's happening is the static electricity that has built up in your hair is attracted to the static electricity in the balloon.

Try shuffling your feet on a carpet and then touching a doorknob. *Zap!* You get a shock. If the lights were off, you would see a spark jump from your hand to the knob. This time static electricity is building up in your hand from the action of rubbing your shoes on the carpet. It is attracted to the static electricity that has built up in the doorknob. When you touch the doorknob,

TRY THIS only if supervised by an adult

Here are a couple of simple experiments you can try with balloons to see the effects of static electricity.

Blow up a few balloons and tie knots on the ends. Rub a couple of the balloons against a wool sweater. In this way, you are charging up the balloons with static electricity. Test what happens when you put a "charged up" balloon on the wall, or the ceiling, or even your arm. When you let go it should stick to the wall, the ceiling—and even to you!

Now take another balloon and rub it against a wool sweater. Hold this "charged up" balloon near a small stream of water from your faucet. The water should bend toward the balloon.

the buildup of static electricity is released.

During a thunderstorm, the same thing happens in the cumulonimbus cloud, only the spark is much, much bigger.

In a Flash

Lightning strikes can occur on the ground, in the air, between two clouds, and within one cloud. It just depends on where the static electricity builds up the strongest. In cloud-to-ground lightning strikes, for example, the static electricity in the cloud is attracted to the electricity on the ground. When the attraction between the cloud and the ground grows strong enough, the electricity in the cloud moves toward the ground. This charged air lights up as it approaches the ground. At the same time as this light gets close to the ground, electricity simultaneously moves from the ground up. This is called the return stroke. Eventually the light flashes meet and—*Crack! Boom!*—the sky lights up.

Although scientists know a lot about lightning and agree that thunder clouds are filled with electrical energy that causes lightning bolts to occur, they don't fully understand how the process works.

Did You Know?

Lightning can be seen from space? Photographs from space show faint flashes of lightning coming from the tops of clouds. These are called red sprites or bluejets.

Types of Lightning

Lightning strikes can be as much as five miles in length. Although the flash may look wide, it may actually be as thin as a pencil. It's the hot, glowing air surrounding the jagged strike that makes it look larger.

All lightning strikes are streaks—that is single zigzag strokes. They may look very different, however, to the human eye. Lightning types include: sheet, ribbon, bead, ball, and fork. For instance, sheet lightning is the name for lightning that occurs inside a cloud. The whole cloud gets very bright and looks like a giant white sheet. The jagged stroke occurs, but it's invisible to the human eye.

In ribbon lighting, the lightning's return flash separates from the main stroke, thus creating a side streak that gives the lightning the look of a ribbon.

Sometimes the brightness along the lightning's path is uneven and gives the stroke the look of beads or pearls along a string. This is very rare. It is called bead lightning, or pearl-necklace lightning.

Some people have reported seeing glowing balls of light in thunderstorms, which disappear after a few seconds. This is called ball lightning. Scientists don't know yet how or why these form. On occasion, some people have mistaken them for UFOs.

The Sound of the Gods Battling

What is it about lightning that makes so much noise? Actually, it's similar to what happens when a balloon is burst with a sharp pin. The air inside the balloon expands, or flies outward, suddenly. The air essentially explodes, causing a shock wave in the air which makes a loud *bang*.

When lightning flashes, the air it travels through heats up to about 50,000°F. When air heats up this quickly it also expands very rapidly, causing loud shock waves, and—*boom!*—thunder.

Why does thunder make a rumbling and rolling sound sometimes and a sharp crack and crackling sound others? The fact is, thunder makes a variety of sounds. When a single large bolt strikes very close by, the sound is a very loud *clap!* If many smaller bolts strike or if a single strike is far away, rumbling sounds will result. In general, the larger the energy of the explosion, the lower or deeper the sound.

How Close Is That Storm?

Because sound travels so much slower than light, we hear thunder after we see lightning. By counting the number of seconds between a lightning strike and the sound of thunder, you can tell how far away the strike is. A five-second pause indicates that the lightning is about one mile away. Ten seconds indicates it's two miles away, and so on. This is called the flash-to-bang method of measuring. It is a pretty accurate way of telling how far away lightning is. Try it next time a thunder-storm occurs near you.

Have you ever watched a lightning storm on a summer night but not heard thunder? It doesn't mean there isn't thunder, it just means that you're too far away to hear it. This kind of lightning is called heat lightning.

Destructive Forces

Lightning is both beautiful and exciting to watch. It's also very destructive, though in the long run, beneficial to the health of the planet.

Did You Know?

Lightning strikes aren't all bad. Some strikes can produce nitrogen, which helps plants to grow.

Lightning near Williston, North Dakota, in 1992

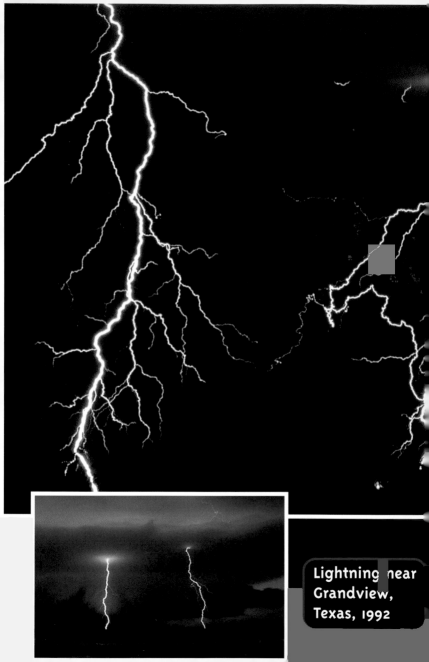

Lightning near
Grandview,
Texas, 1992

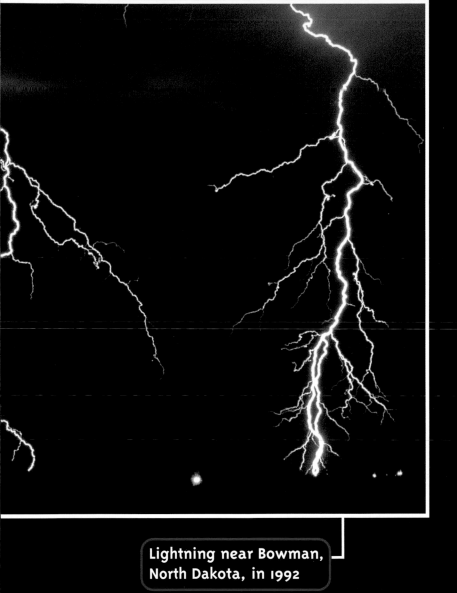

Lightning near Bowman,
North Dakota, in 1992

Lightning near the Palo Duro Canyon, Texas, in 1977

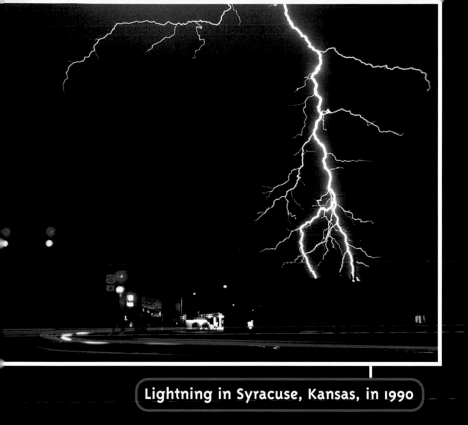

Lightning in Syracuse, Kansas, in 1990

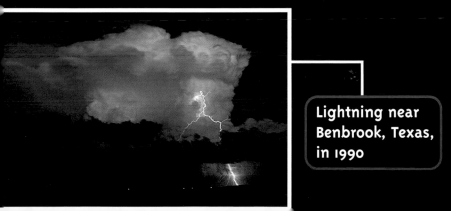

Lightning near Benbrook, Texas, in 1990

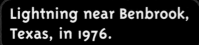

Lightning near Benbrook,
Texas, in 1976.

Thunderclouds
approaching
Dallas, Texas,
in 1976

Thunderstorm approaching
Benbrook, Texas, in 1976

Thunderclouds near Syracuse, Kansas, in 1990

Lightning near Walter, Oklahoma, in 1990

How Dangerous Is Lightning?

Lightning can cause damage in a number of ways. One is by directly striking objects on the ground. As a rule, lightning is drawn to the tallest object in a clearing.

Have you ever come across a burnt tree in a forest? It may well have been hit by lightning. Lightning can set whole forests on fire. This type of fire is actually part of the natural life cycle of a forest or field environment. Fire burns up old vegetation and makes room for new trees and plants to grow.

Surprisingly, most trees that are hit by lightning may be damaged but not necessarily killed—at least not immediately. Burn scars are the telltale signs of a strike. After lightning hits a tree, the bark is usually splintered and weakened, giving hungry bark beetles a chance to attack the tree from the inside. Eventually, the tree dies.

Lightning and Your Home

Lightning can strike houses. The parts that are high up in the air, such as roofs and antennas, are hit most often. Lightning may start fires inside houses or cause **electrical shocks** that travel through walls or electrical circuits. Sparks can even fly out of electrical circuits and outlets. Wires in most homes are **grounded**, meaning connected to the ground, so that lightning's electricity moves directly from the house to the ground. Remember never to use electrical appliances during a thunderstorm—including the telephone.

When Lightning Strikes Cars, Airplanes, and Rockets

Generally, you are safer inside a car during a thunderstorm than outside of it. If a car is hit, electricity will flow through the metal and not touch the people inside. If you're in a car during a thunderstorm, roll up the windows and don't touch any metal objects.

Airplanes are largely made of metal. What happens, then, if a plane is struck by lightning? If a plane is on the ground, just as is the case with cars, the people inside are safe as long as they don't touch any metal.

But if a plane is in the air, it's a different story. Flying planes that are hit by lightning do get damaged. Lightning can create small holes or burns in planes' metal skin. In a few cases, lightning has caused airplanes to crash. Most times, though, planes keep flying. In general, airplanes in thunderstorms are at greater risk from wind and low visibility than from strikes of lightning.

Rockets can create lightning when they fly through clouds. As the rocket speeds through, it rubs against the water drops or ice crystals in the surrounding clouds, which causes static electricity to build up in the rocket. The plane's static electricity is attracted to the clouds' static electricity. The Apollo 12 spacecraft was struck twice by lightning it created itself when traveling through a cumulonimbus cloud.

Extreme Danger:
People Hit by Lightning

If the wind is increasing, lightning is flashing, thunder is rumbling, and static is on the radio, look out! Although weather forecasters are usually able to predict when thunderstorms are coming, people don't always take cover and every year some are struck by lightning.

Most people who are hit are not actually

struck directly, but instead receive an electrical shock from a lightning strike near by. Contrary to what some believe, people do not burst into flames or turn into a pile of ashes. Nor do they become charged up with electricity and dangerous to touch. In fact, the electrical charges pass right out of bodies. The shock to the human system, however, can be very severe. In the end, though, most people do eventually recover from lightning strikes.

Nathan's Story

Nathan, from Illinois, is one of the luckier survivors. Here's what he has recounted about his experience:

"I was indirectly struck by lightning on Friday, August 23, 1996, in the three-car garage attached to my home. I was thirteen years old at the time and it was three days before I started eighth grade. At about 6 P.M. my mom left to take my twin seven-year-old brother and sister Brandon and Erika to a birthday party. I stayed home with my nine-year-old brother Matthew. A few minutes after my mom left, she called me on the car phone and said it looked like a storm was coming. The sky looked green like a tornado was coming, and she told me to take Matthew and hurry to the basement. She said to stay in the back room, away from windows and stay off the phone. I asked her if I could go into the garage to bring the cats in the house and she said 'Okay, but hurry.' I went into the garage and found one cat. I was barefoot and had on jeans and a T-shirt, but no belt. As I was looking for the other cat, the metal garage door blew open. When I touched the doorknob to close it, I was struck. I couldn't let go of the door-knob for a short time. I saw a blue zigzagging on the door and also saw it go into my right hand, up my arm, across my chest, and out my left shoulder. I was thrown back into the workbench chair, and fell. I don't think I lost consciousness. My arms were numb, my chest hurt, and there was a terrible smell. I went to the door to go back into the house, but waited because I was afraid I would get shocked if I touched that doorknob. My arms were numb and I could hardly lift my hand to open the door. When I went in I told Matthew to call 911 because I thought I had just been electrocuted. He thought I was teasing him until I took off my shirt and he saw that my chest and arms were burnt.

I was sitting on the couch when the ambulance and two paramedics arrived. They weren't sure, but from what I told them they said they thought I had been struck by lightning. When my mom called, Matthew told her that I had been electrocuted. When we got to the hospital, they checked my heart, took X-rays and checked my kidneys, but couldn't find anything wrong. My arms were still numb, but I was slowly starting to feel normal again, and the burns started going away. I was told that it was called flash burns. After three hours in the emergency room I was sent home with a note for school saying, 'Struck by lightning—may return to school with 2 Tylenol every 4 hours as needed for pain.'

My sixth-grade teacher told our class one time that you have a better chance of being struck by lightning than winning the lottery. My mom bought me five lottery tickets that night and you know what? You do have a better chance of being struck by lightning!"

Nathan's account was obtained by the Lightning Strike and Electric Shock Survivors International (LS&ESSI). They are a worldwide support group for people who have survived lightning strikes or who have been injured by electricity. More first-hand accounts of such experiences can be found on their World Wide Web site at:

http://www.mindspring.com/~lightningstrike

Did You Know?

A few people who have been struck by lightning claim miraculous changes in their lives. Some report having been cured of blindness, others of deafness or illness. Still others have said they became smarter. None of these claims has been proven to be true. What is known, however, is that severe damage—and sometimes death—can occur.

The Dangers of Lightning

People who have been hit repeatedly by lightning are nicknamed "human **lightning rods**." These people are not special, they are just hanging out in the wrong places! One United States National Park Ranger, has survived seven lightning strikes. People aren't the only ones to get hit by lightning—cattle, horses, dogs, pigs, cats, birds and anything else outdoors during a thunderstorm can be hit.

Some people have been severely hurt or even killed by lightning. Golfers on open golf courses, farmers driving tractors in open fields, swimmers and other people in open water, are all among those most likely to be hit by lightning. That's because metal and water are good **conductors** of electricity, meaning electricity easily moves through them. So if you're caught outside in a storm, be sure to stay away from water and metal during thunderstorms.

Trees should also be avoided. In fact most lightning deaths occur when people stand too close to trees during thunderstorms. Dangers are many including being struck by lightning, burned, or crushed by falling branches.

Tim's Story

Here's what Tim, a Canadian college student, recalls about his experience:

"I was struck by lightning on July 3, 1993, when three of my friends and I decided to go on a camping trip to Algonquin Provincial Park in Ontario, Canada. While sleeping in my tent I was awoken by the sound of thunder that shook the ground. In a short but extremely violent thunderstorm, I was struck by lightning.

I was unconscious for about ten minutes and when I came to, I was completely disoriented. I had absolutely no sense of direction, could not feel or move my limbs, was completely deaf, and for the most part couldn't see past ten feet.

For the next eight hours, while we waited for an emergency military rescue, my body was in a state of shock. I felt very numb and consciousness was a struggle.

Obviously I survived, but the strike did not leave me unharmed. I am permanently deaf in one ear and have to use a hearing aid in the other. I also received minor, permanent nerve damage to my spine, have diminished eyesight, unstable balance, and several scars on my body. One of the most interesting scars (if a scar can be considered interesting) is a thin black ring around my neck caused by the vaporization of a gold chain I had been wearing.

What is most important about my experience is the change my life took afterwards. You see, as I lay in the mud shortly after I was hit, I truly believed I would die. When I realized that I was going to live, my entire outlook on life changed. For several weeks after the strike, I was very sick but at the same time, I was extremely content. I was stone deaf for at least two months, but during that time I was so happy to be alive and I was very optimistic about the future."

Web site addresses

There are many places on the Internet where information can be found about lightning.

The Weather Channel home page is an excellent source of up-to-date weather forecasts and late-breaking news about severe weather, including thunderstorms, lightning, tornadoes, and hurricanes. You can find it at:

http://www.weather.com

By clicking on "Safety Tips" on The Weather Channel home page, you will "surf" to a site under the heading of PROJECT SafeSide. These pages provide interesting information about specific severe weather events, including lightning. PROJECT SafeSide was created by The Weather Channel in conjunction with the American Red Cross. You can also go directly to that site:

http://www.weather.com/safeside/

Tim's story appears on the Web site called "Cori's Lightning Links," which has some of the best lightning photography on the internet. The address for this site is:

http://www.prazen.com/cori/links.html

For more information about lightning safety, you can visit the Web site called "Be Lightning Wise" that was put together by the Boy Scouts of America. Their Internet address is:

http://www.usscouts.org/gold/safe_lig.html

Another very good site for weather-related information is the "Eye on the World—Violent Planet Page." Besides providing facts, stories, photographs, and satellite images, this page also has links to many other sites. The address for this site is:

http://www.iwaynet.net/%7Ekwroejr/violent.html

Thunderstorm Safety

Safety is very important. If you follow these simple rules, you will keep yourself and whomever you are with *much* safer.

The most important rule is simply this: If a thunderstorm is approaching, get inside.

If thunder and lightning are very near and you don't have time to get inside, follow these rules:

1. If you feel your hair stand up on end, quickly drop to a crouched position, bend forward, keep your feet close together, and place your hands on your knees. Get as close to the ground as possible, but try to keep as little of your body in contact with the ground as you can. Be absolutely sure to keep your head off the ground. Never lie flat on the ground.

2. Get away from trees or other tall objects.

3. Stay away from hilltops, benches, and open fields and seek shelter in a low-lying area, such as a ditch or ravine.

4. If you are with a group of people, spread out.

5. Stay away from water.

6. Stay away from metal objects such as bikes, fences, poles, and umbrellas.

7. Remove metal objects like jewelry, coins, and barrettes from yourself.

If you are indoors during a thunderstorm:

1. Stay away from electrical sockets, appliances, television, and telephones. Do not use water or anything connected to water.

2. Stay away from windows and doors.

3. If possible, avoid being in isolated sheds or buildings.

4. Protect electrical appliances by unplugging the electrical cords beforehand.

A person who is struck by lightning may be temporarily paralyzed. Often, however, he can be revived. If a victim isn't breathing or his heart isn't beating, quickly call for emergency help.

Remember, thunderstorms and lightning can be fascinating, but make sure you're safe and sound before sitting back and enjoying their many wonders.

Glossary

ATMOSPHERE—The layers of air that surround the earth.

CONDUCTOR—An object or substance such as metal or water that allows electricity to move through it.

CUMULONIMBUS—Also called a thunderhead. A puffy type of cloud that towers high in the sky.

CUMULUS—Fluffy, cottony clouds that are usually seen in good weather.

ELECTRICAL SHOCK—Shock caused by strong electricity passing through a body. A person experiencing electric shock may stop breathing and his heart may stop beating. The longer the contact with electricity, the smaller the chance of survival.

GROUNDING—A method of guiding electricity away from a building or person into the ground. This is often done by attaching wires to a lightning rod on one end and placing the other end in the ground.

HAIL—These frozen chunks of ice form during thunderstorms when very strong drafts of wind inside cumulonimbus clouds push water drops higher and higher up into the air where they freeze because of the cold temperatures. The ice crystals then fall and are pushed up again and refrozen. This happens over and over again until the ice crystals grow too heavy to be held up by the wind and fall to the ground as hail.

LIGHTNING—A flash of electricity in the sky, usually generated during a thunderstorm.

LIGHTNING ROD—A metal pole placed on the highest part of a building. The pole is connected by grounding wires to the ground so that it will lead the electricity of a lightning bolt safely away from the building and into the ground.

METEOROLOGIST—A person who studies weather. By looking at what is happening in the atmosphere, meteorologists predict the weather.

STATIC ELECTRICITY—Electricity that stays in one place. It builds up until a spark is triggered. In contrast, current electricity is electricity that flows and is used, among other things, to power electric lights.

STORM CHASERS—People who try to get as close as possible to severe weather systems, such as thunderstorms, tornadoes, and hurricanes, in order to study them.

THUNDER—The sound created when the air

around a lightning stroke is heated and expands at very high speeds.

THUNDERSTORM—Severe storm that can be accompanied by heavy rain, hail, strong winds, thunder, and lightning.

TORNADO—A dangerous, rotating funnel cloud that can produce winds of over 200 miles per hour.

INDEX